GRUMPY CAT
Coloring Book

John Kurtz

Dover Publications
Garden City, New York

Grumpy Cat™

Grumpy Cat and Related Artwork © and ® Grumpy Cat Limited
www.GrumpyCats.com Used Under License

Bibliographical Note

Spot-the-Differences Grumpy Cat Coloring Book is a new work, first
published by Dover Publications in 2017.

International Standard Book Number

ISBN-13: 978-0-486-81959-4
ISBN-10: 0-486-81959-0

Manufactured in the United States by LSC Communications Book LLC
81959002   2021
www.doverpublications.com

Someone is looking mighty grumpy in the 27 puzzles featured in this little activity book. Grumpy Cat knows that even though the two renderings of each of the puzzles look the same, someone has altered the image on the right side so that it is slightly different from the original image on the left side. Grumpy Cat doesn't like anyone messing with the photos! Can you help Grumpy Cat spot the five changes in each puzzle? Try your best to find the differences, but if you get stuck, just turn to the Solutions section, which begins on page 56. When you are finished, you can color the pages, where you'll see Grumpy Cat sulking, yet putting up with a variety of not-so-unpleasant activities!

2

3

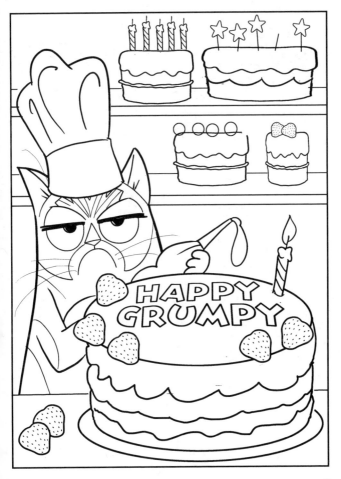

HAPPY
GRUMPY

8

14

19

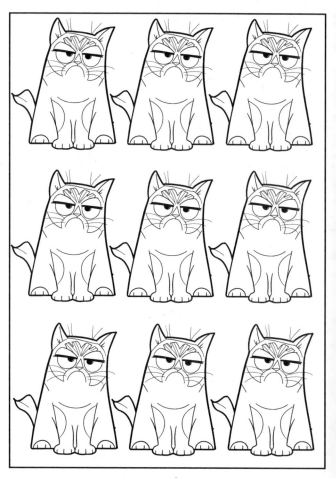

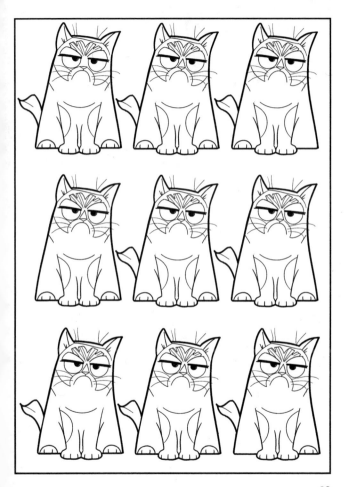

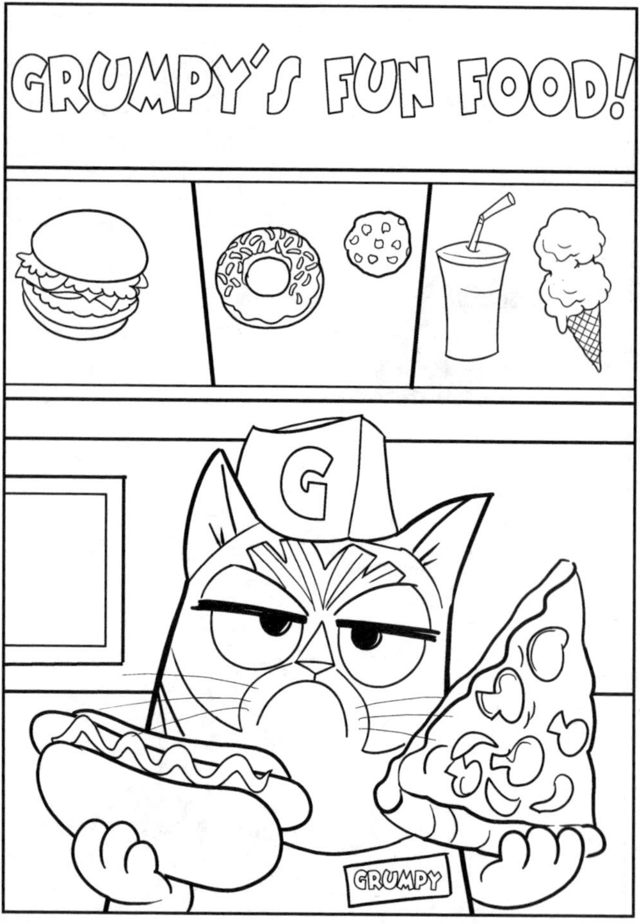
GRUMPY'S FUN FOOD!
G
GRUMPY

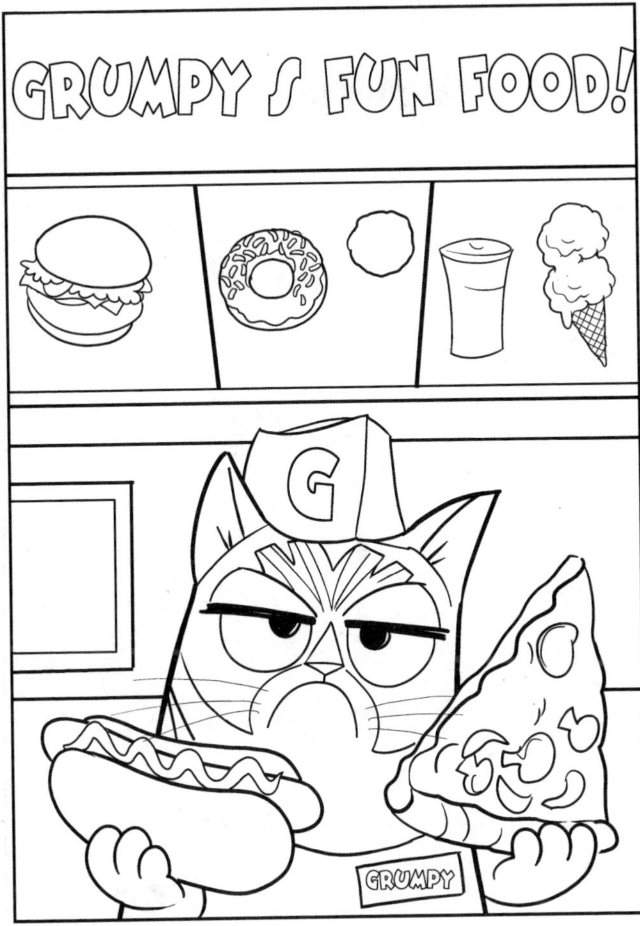
GRUMPY S FUN FOOD!
G
GRUMPY

42

45

47

51

52

Solutions

page 3

page 5

page 7

page 9

page 11

page 13

page 15

page 17

page 19

page 21

page 23

page 25

page 27

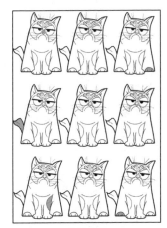

page 29

page 31

page 33

page 35

page 37

page 39

page 41

page 43

page 45

page 47

page 49

page 51

page 53

page 55